MURDER AT THE NO-KILL ANIMAL SHELTER

Judith Ayn

BookLocker
Saint Petersburg, Florida

Print ISBN: 978-1-64719-356-0
Epub ISBN: 978-1-64719-357-7
Mobi ISBN: 978-1-64719-358-4

Published by BookLocker.com, Inc., St. Petersburg, Florida.

Printed on acid-free paper.

The characters and events in this book are fictitious. Any similarity to real persons, living or dead, is coincidental and not intended by the author.

BookLocker.com, Inc.
2021

First Edition

Library of Congress Cataloguing in Publication Data
Ayn, Judith
MURDER AT THE NO-KILL ANIMAL SHELTER by Judith Ayn
Library of Congress Control Number: 2021902176

Dedication

To my son, my heart, John Brian, and to the many cats who have
owned me over the years: Blackie #1, Blackie #2, and my current
felines Ziggy and Sammy, the models for Fred and Ethel. Thank you
for all the love and support. You all have rescued me!

Chapter One

The only spot of color in the muddied driveway near the kennels, or what remained of them, was a blue tarp under the body. Cheater's Lake Homicide Detective Mark Walsh knelt on the wet ground, then bent closer to examine the old man's bearded face.

"This is Carson Butts," Officer Sharon Laskey said in a loud voice to be heard over the nearby fire truck engines. "The caretaker for the shelter according to one of the witnesses." She scraped mud from her boots on a nearby rock.

Walsh rose to his full six-four height and surveyed the area. The small soggy yard contained two run-down wooden buildings, reduced to little more than their foundations. Further down the driveway closer to the road stood a tiny brick house with a large Cheater's Lake Animal Rescue sign across its upper front.

Wisps of gray ash swirled in the air as a soft but steady rain fell. Springtime in Washington state, weather-wise the same as summer, fall and winter.

"There doesn't seem to be a mark on him. How'd he die?"

"Maybe smoke inhalation from the fire?" Laskey stepped aside as a firefighter deftly wrangled a huge hose and dragged it back to one of the trucks. She pulled a glove off and retied her light brown hair through the back of a Mariners baseball cap. Shorter than Walsh and a few years younger than his early thirties, Laskey was dressed in dark jeans and a waterproof jacket. Grocery shopping when dispatch called her to the scene, there'd been no time to change.

Across from the burned structures a variety of cars, trucks and vans lined up. Volunteers struggled with cages and carriers loading dogs, cats, birds, rabbits and other orphans for transport. Creatures complained in barks, meows and hisses, while a few voices shouted directions.

"Where do the animals go now?" Walsh asked.

Laskey sighed. "To other shelters within a hundred miles. As if these poor things weren't traumatized enough being here. Dammit! What kind of monster burns down an animal refuge trying to help unwanted pets? And why kill an old caretaker?"

"Questions we get to answer." Walsh nodded in the direction of crime scene personnel working the grounds.

"While they gather evidence, let's check behind the buildings."

The two of them walked around the back of the kennels and followed a swampy path into thick woods. After a few minutes slog through the muck, they came upon a tiny clearing. A rough campsite set up with a circle of stones for a cook fire also contained a beat-up aluminum pan nearby. In addition, a tattered one-man pup tent and neon yellow sleeping bag were stashed against a tree trunk. Their search turned up no campers in the area.

Before they headed back, Laskey snapped photos with her phone and noted the GPS coordinates. "Why camp here?"

Walsh shook his head. "Add it to the other mysteries. The techs can check this out, too." He shivered as raindrops slid inside his collar. "Let's get out of here."

***

A half mile away from the fire scene, DM Collins, founder and director of the animal rescue, sat at the kitchen table of her cozy cedar-clad ranch home. As she sipped black coffee from an oversize mug embossed *Animal Rescue Rocks*, her German shepherd, Henry, rested his large black head on her feet.

Someone killed her gentle caretaker and destroyed the animal refuge she'd worked so hard to establish. She was determined that someone would be caught and punished if it took every dime DM had to make that happen. And thanks to her late husband, there were many, many dimes in her bank account.

Was this personal? DM ran through a list of enemies she'd made over the years. Admittedly, a short one, but no one got through life unscathed. She didn't plan to offer names to the police until she'd investigated on her own.

So, was this all done to make a political point? An animal extremist group looking for publicity? But what point could they make? That unwanted animals shouldn't be saved? And why both arson and murder?

DM refilled her cup. Could an enemy of Carson's be the culprit? Again, he'd lived and worked on the property for a decade, so why would someone kill him now?

***

The woman's attention turned to the strikingly handsome Detective Walsh seated across from her. Thick dark hair, blue eyes, strong jaw. She was forty-plus and he was easily a decade younger but definitely yummy. Unfortunately, this was not the time for flirting.

Walsh didn't waste time on small talk. "Ms. Collins, what do you know about your caretaker, Mr. Butts?"

"It's DM, Detective. Carson worked at the shelter from the time I opened it. Very quiet guy, no outside life. I hired him to clean the kennels at first, but he was so good with the animals, he eventually became the all-around caretaker."

Laskey stirred her coffee. "How did he apply for the job?"

"He didn't actually apply. He just showed up during construction and we began talking. I liked him and decided to give him a try." DM rose and brought a plate of pastries to the table.

"Is that how you usually hire employees?" Walsh asked, eyebrow raised. He bit into an apple turnover. Delicious.

DM laughed. "You might not approve, Detective, but I'm generally right-on about the people I hire. Anyway, I can't add much about Carson. He never left the property and didn't have any visitors. His only hobby that I know of was fishing on Sunday mornings."

"Do you know where he lived before, where he came from?" Laskey's pen was poised over her notebook.

"Nope, sorry. A slight accent that sounded Southern, but he never talked about himself and I didn't push. As I said, he was good with the animals, and that's always been my major concern with people I hire."

Walsh changed the subject. "How far does your land extend from the shelter?"

"I own sixty acres. Have you found something on the property?"

Officer Laskey leaned closer to DM and thumbed her cell. "Somebody's camping about a half mile from the shelter. Did you give permission for that?"

She swiped the campsite scenes. "No. I don't recognize anything here."

Walsh uncrossed his long legs. "Our crime scene people have been out there. So far, it appears to be a lone camper. This stretch of land seems pretty deserted, except for your shelter and this house."

"I know and that's why I bought it, for the peace and quiet of the woods. The only drawback for me living in the Pacific Northwest is the days are short in the spring and it gets dark so early." DM switched on another lamp. "I don't understand what happened at the shelter, none of it."

"Do you have anywhere else you could stay?" Laskey asked as she put her phone away. "This house may not be safe for you."

DM sighed and pointed to Henry, fully alert and standing in front of her. "I have protection, so I'll be fine."

"Can you think of anyone at all who has a grudge against you? Any social media trolls?" Walsh asked.

"No, Detective." She rubbed her eyes. "People are more upset with the high-kill shelters. A no-kill shelter costs a lot more to run because virtually every animal is promised a home till they can be fostered, adopted or pass away. Social media hasn't been a worry for us. We use it for adoptions all the time."

Walsh and Laskey asked a few more questions then left DM to her musings.

***

The arsonist took a long hot shower. He changed into sweats, grabbed a cold beer and plopped onto his faux leather recliner. His lip curled as he thought of Collins. Bitch got what she deserved. He picked up an oily rag and methodically cleaned several guns on the battered coffee table.

As he washed his hands, of course, his cell rang. "Yup." He grabbed a dish towel to dry off and put the call on speaker.

"You idiot!" a man's shouted voice. "The caretaker died. Simple arson's murder now."

"I didn't kill him! He got in the way, Tony. He came at my back when I was pouring the gasoline, trying to stop me. I punched him and he fell on the ground, out cold. Since he couldn't see my face under the mask, I left him there. The fire did the job. I expect the money in my account within the hour."

The voice was so loud it echoed around the living room. "I told you before — don't use names on the phone! Who camped out close to the shelter? Did you miss that little detail, too?"

"What? What are you talking about? There wasn't anyone else around." He kicked the edge of the table. "Goddammit!"

"Well, there was, moron. So, don't expect the second half of your payment just yet. You gotta make sure you didn't leave a boy scout witness out there." The call ended.

***

Walsh and Laskey met in the Cheater's Lake PD conference room. The two examined printouts after they grabbed sandwiches and hot drinks.

"I have a friend, Greg Hogan, retired San Diego PD, who's opening a PI business. He's looking into the background of the deceased caretaker as a favor to me. All we know so far, he's got no criminal history." Walsh pinned a driver's license photo of Butts on the wall's whiteboard.

Laskey opened a bag of chips. "In the meantime, the medical examiner promised a report by tomorrow."

Walsh took a couple of sheets of paper from Laskey and opened the blinds in the room. "What'd you find on Collins? Besides the local scuttlebutt because she's wealthy."

"Daisy Marigold," Laskey laughed, "was brought up in Oregon by parents who lived off the grid, homeschooled, etc. When she turned eighteen, she fled to the big city of Seattle, met a much older man and married him. After a few years, he developed inoperable cancer, leaving her a very well-off widow."

Walsh pinned Collins' current driver's license photo on the board. She was a redhead with green eyes. The picture didn't do justice to the attractive, petite woman they'd interviewed. He might ask her out after the case was closed.

"DM, legal name change, got into animal welfare." Laskey popped a peanut butter cookie in her mouth and tossed her paper plate in the trash. "At first, she financially backed a vet clinic and private shelter, then built the no-kill she runs now. Along the way, she bought a bunch of real estate in Washington state, most of it rural and undeveloped. She's pioneered prison programs for therapy dog training and has another site on her land planned out for classes on personal security animals. That's due to open sometime soon."

"We'll have to search for any large insurance policies on the place. Any unhappy step-children or business partners gunning for her?" Walsh asked.

"No one's surfaced yet. I'll keep checking." Laskey drained the last of the coffee pot.

"It's too early for the Fire Marshal's report, although the chief told me he suspects arson. Evidence techs have their hands full. Let's split this pile and sift through the 911 calls and witness statements." Walsh filled his cup with hot water and dropped in a teabag.

They walked back to their offices to search for more answers on the mysterious Mr. Butts and the fire.

Chapter Two

In the early morning hours before dawn, two cats awoke to loud sounds at the opening end of their cave. A man dragged himself inside, slumped against one of the walls and swore as he wedged himself into place. A few minutes later, noise from his nose rattled the air.

Orange Cat padded quietly over to the rumpled form. The man smelled like fire and something else that made her one eye water. Suddenly, he sat up and noticed her.

"Get away from me or I'll break your neck!" he yelled. He threw a rock in her direction, spit and laid back down again. Soon the rattling noise resumed.

The kitten fled to Gray Cat and hid behind him. When nighttime came, the man was gone.

Chapter Three

Detective Walsh switched off his pickup truck's engine. The animal shelter grounds were covered in several inches of thick mud thanks to days of constant rain. Walsh's boots pulled with each step as he methodically checked around the burned buildings, then headed behind them for another look into the surrounding woods.

No useful evidence had been recovered at the deserted campsite he and Laskey discovered, but he had a strange feeling they all missed something. He circled the same site, but nothing special drew his attention.

Walsh sighed, pulled his waterproof hood tighter. He slipped and slid as he followed a narrow deer path deeper into thick stands of trees and brush. The wind lessened and eerie sounds floated on the air from a northerly direction. For half an hour he pushed on, then emerged from the trees into a place full of rocks and boulders. No signs of camping, but the noise he'd heard was more distinct. Howling, animals in distress.

After a few more minutes, Walsh investigated a small slit between two giant boulders and found a cave. He lowered his head and half-crept inside. Pitiful crying echoed and two pairs of green eyes blinked when the police flashlight penetrated the darkness. Momentary silence.

Two lumps, one small, one much larger. Both drenched, gray black with soot, shivering. Somehow weak, yet furious enough to hiss and spit when he approached.

"Hey, guys." Walsh used his softest voice. "You'll be okay. There's still animal people from the shelter who can help you." He reached for the smaller lump first, rewarded for his efforts with a razor-sharp swipe which bloodied his hand.

A string of loud curses followed. The cats backed themselves further against the stone walls. "I can't believe you did that!" Walsh used tissues to stem the bleeding. "You can't stay here, so like it or not, I'm getting you out." He took a deep breath and calmed himself.

The detective grabbed the smaller cat by the scruff of the neck and placed it in his jacket pocket. The cat half-heartedly struggled as Walsh zipped the pocket mostly closed. Then he removed the jacket, set it on the stone floor and shrugged off his down vest. The larger cat fought valiantly but was soon swathed securely in the vest and held against Walsh's chest. The rain jacket back on, the threesome left the cave huddled together for the long slog back to Walsh's truck.

***

A short drive away from the shelter, Walsh rang the doorbell of Director DM Collins' home. In his arms he clutched a small box with crudely punched air holes. Beside his feet sat a similar box, three times larger than the first.

She held the door open and motioned Walsh inside. Once he'd set the boxes on the floor, she handed him a cup of coffee. "Is there news about Carson or the fire?"

Walsh shook his head. "Not yet. Can someone take these two cats? They look kind of rough." He gently slid the makeshift carriers over to her with his foot.

She moved across the room, away from him and the boxes, to a floral couch. "Where did you find them? Never mind. I can't help you." DM pointed to the window overlooking a big yard where a group of dogs played. "With six large dogs crammed in here, cats wouldn't be safe. I'll fix you up with a litter box and food. They can go home with you."

"Me? What I know about cats wouldn't fill a thimble," Walsh protested and rose to leave.

"Then take them to the nearest shelter you can find. I expect they'll be euthanized by tomorrow."

Walsh stared at her. "You'd let them be killed?"

DM shook her head. "I run one of the few no-kill shelters around. Or, I did. Unfortunately, there isn't another one close by anywhere. The others do what they can, but they've got the rest of the animals from my shelter now, too. I can't just this minute miraculously take in more with Carson murdered, the kennels burned down and a criminal investigation that'll tie us up forever." Tears welled in her eyes. "Please, Detective. Take them with you."

Great! Again, what did he know about taking care of cats?

At home, Walsh set the litter box up in his guest bathroom. He filled two small bowls with canned slop, another with dry food and a big bowl full of water. Both cats disappeared as soon as he opened their cardboard carriers. Muttering to himself about felines in general, he took a shower and dropped into bed.

Chapter Four

From his CLPD office a few days later, Walsh called Greg. "I need help. I ended up with two stray cats and no one will take them off my hands."

Greg laughed. "You're hopeless, Markie. A big, tough homicide detective with two little pussycats. Outnumbered?"

"Lucky for you we're fifteen hundred miles apart, buddy. I'm in a mood to shoot you between the eyes."

"What have they done to you?" Greg continued to laugh. "Destroyed your house?"

Walsh yawned. "They hide all day and play all night. I can't find them, but they eat like it's their last meal and poop like elephants. Their special food costs three times more than a steak and I'm constantly sweeping up kitty litter. I practically had a heart attack when the big one jumped on my chest in the middle of the night." He held the phone away from his ear as Greg laughed even louder.

"What have you named 'em?"

"I'm not naming them, I'm not keeping them. I tried to give the pair to DM, the shelter's director, but she blew me off. She's sexy as hell but won't give an inch when it comes to people rescuing animals. I think she figured me for a sucker."

"Tell me more about this director person," Greg said. "I've wondered if there were any females up in the north country you'd find acceptable."

"Acceptable? She's got red hair she wears loose, floats around her shoulders, and green eyes. Nice figure and very smart. But she's at the heart of this crazy case, so definitely off limits." Walsh sighed.

"Hang in there, Markie, you're overdue for some luck in the romance department." Greg chuckled.

"Right. Anyway, I've gotta go. Thanks for the support." Walsh ended the call and frowned. "No way these cats are staying."

***

Later that afternoon, Walsh and Laskey met again in the conference room to review the animal shelter case. "According to the medical examiner, the caretaker, Mr. Butts, was injected with a fatal dosage of Ketamine," Walsh said. "Either he was the intended victim and this was a planned murder, or maybe in the wrong place at the wrong time for the arson." He sat at the table and removed his suit jacket.

"Special K they call it," Laskey flipped through the case notebook. "Vets use it to calm animals. Human predators like it for date rape. The problem is dosing can be tricky, especially with any pre-existing health conditions. The killer had to be familiar with the drug and either bring it with him or know how to access it at the shelter."

Walsh nodded. "Our victim had heart problems, so that was a bonus. Did the killer know that, or was he just lucky? We're back to square one. Why would someone murder Mr. Butts? My PI friend is still digging but so far *nada*. Got any theories?"

Laskey moved over to the whiteboard and tapped the photo of Butts. "You think he could've been in Witness Protection or something?"

"Hmm...that's an interesting idea to pursue. In the meantime, I called the state prison where Collins opened the program for dog training. The warden gave me a list of names of disgruntled prisoners who washed out and a couple who were never chosen to participate. It's thin, I admit, but this feels personal to me." He slid half the stack of pages over to her.

"We know the fire was arson." Laskey took a slice of pepperoni pizza from the box on the table. She handed Walsh a can of Pepsi and napkins as he helped himself to the steaming pie. "But Collins had plenty of insurance, so what's to gain except nuisance?"

"A statement that he can get to her anywhere, anytime and destroy what she's worked for? His own hatred of animals?" Walsh gave Laskey another printed list. "Ms. Collins faxed over every employee's name and contact info, past and present, and the same for volunteers. Get Shawn started on an initial search and we can follow up on any likelys."

Laskey topped off her drink. "We reviewed the 911 calls and witness statements, nothing helpful. There were no cameras, no video. The only forensic evidence are the drugs in poor old Mr. Butts and ashes linked to the arson." She sighed. "Back to more old-fashioned police work."

Chapter Five

"Fred and Ethel? That's what you named your stray cats?" Greg's loud laugh boomed from the cell phone. "You are too strange, Markie. Spending some time down here in laid back San Diego would mellow you out."

"It doesn't matter what you name cats," Mark sighed. "They don't answer to anything or anyone, anyway. The shelter's office reopened after the fire and I stopped by to talk to them. A lady there said it's the tone of voice cats respond to, if they listen at all. That, and of course, the sound of a can opener."

Mark sipped some tea and eyed the two creatures sound asleep on his couch.

"So," Greg said, "tell me again how you ended up like a crazy cat lady."

"Ha, ha. Apparently, these two were being processed by shelter volunteers in the office when all hell broke loose. With the fire and discovery of the caretaker's body, it was so chaotic the cats fled to the woods and hid for a couple days. I found them in a nasty looking cave when I was out walking the crime scene area again. The evidence techs think a human, possibly the perp, was using that place to hide, also.

"How they came into the shelter's orbit is interesting. The big male, gray- striped-tabby, already named Fred, was given up by a librarian who'd just lost her job. She included a yellowed newspaper article touting Fred's part in finding a kidnapped child when she surrendered him."

"The cat solved a crime?" Greg couldn't contain his amusement. "This is just too much good stuff."

"Well, it gets better." Mark pulled a bagel from his toaster and spread it with cream cheese.

"The smaller cat, known as The Cat (TC), ended up at the shelter when one of her owners couldn't take the allergy medication anymore. She's a third Fred's size, an orange calico, with one eye and attitude to spare. TC's history includes a successful attack on a burglar breaking into her former home.

"Anyway, after I took them home and cleaned them up, Fred hid under my bed for two days. Then he begrudgingly allowed petting in return for unlimited food, kitty litter, comfortable sleeping furniture and several battered scratching posts. TC took four days before she stopped hiding and settled down. She's happily joined Fred in the endless eating-sleeping-pooping loop but is skittish about being touched. Every morning I wake up to find she's climbed onto the bed, stretched out on the pillow and draped herself over my head to sleep. Diva doesn't begin to describe the diminutive fur ball.

"I've gotta go in a minute, but here's how I named them. Fred and The Cat didn't sound right. I fell asleep on the couch one night and woke up to an old episode of *I Love Lucy*. Fred and Ethel are legendary."

Greg laughed again. "Okay, I guess that makes sense. I just pictured you up there in soggy Cheater's Lake with a pit bull that likes to hike, not surrounded by two pussycats."

"Maybe not helpful to my macho image, but they do have some law enforcement pedigree. Solving a kidnapping and stopping a burglary. That's more than some rookie cops can claim."

"I'm convinced. Send me a new photo of the beasts when you can. And tell them, welcome to the family." Greg chuckled as he ended the call.

***

Caroline Morris adjusted her Fashion Week onesie outfit, stretched long legs on the chaise lounge in Tony Kurtz's penthouse condo and flipped through piles of color photos. "This one, that one, I don't know," she murmured to herself. Across the living room, her boss and sometime lover typed rapidly on his laptop.

"Babe," she said, "I'm hungry."

Kurtz glared at her. "So, cook something. Don't bother me, I'm busy." He grumbled and reread what he'd just written. One of his big hands slid over his bald head. He regrouped and entered more data.

Caroline huffed and stalked into the chef's kitchen. She selected a pre-made shake from the fridge and sat on a barstool. The floor to ceiling windows of the Seattle skyscraper made her dizzy, but at least it was pouring rain and the lights were muted.

"So, what's next for your *real* girlfriend, DM?" Caroline asked in a whiny voice. "Gonna have dumbo Art-the-Arsonist kidnap her favorite dog?"

Kurtz vaulted out of his desk chair and grabbed Caroline by the throat. As the woman struggled to breathe, he shook her. "You were hired to take pictures. Just shut up and do it." He finally released her and she slid against the granite-covered island to the floor. "I'm not telling you again."

Caroline gasped for air. No job or man was worth this. She'd be gone for good the minute he left the condo to meet Art or one of his other lackeys. Luckily, all she had to pack was her toothbrush.

Chapter Six

Cheater's Lake Police Chief Terrence Riley called the press conference to order and introduced Detective Walsh, who stood behind him in the station's conference room.

"As you know, there was a fire at the Cheater's Lake Animal Rescue a few days ago. The shelter's caretaker, Carson Butts, did not survive and we are pursuing his death as a homicide. The fire has also been determined arson. Detective Walsh will fill in more details."

Walsh moved to the podium. "We have a person of interest we need to interview — a camper on the shelter's land, there on or before the time of the fire. Anyone with information about this event or the camper is asked to contact our Crime Stoppers line, where you will remain anonymous. Although there was extensive damage to the shelter's property, no animals were hurt. The investigation is ongoing."

Riley frowned at Walsh's short and sweet speech. Under his breath, so only Walsh could hear, he said, "Big shot detective from Phoenix. Could you spare all those words?" He took back the mike and rambled on about the department until reporters began to stir.

"We will update you in the next few days," Riley promised as members of the press hurried out the door.

"Get this thing solved, Walsh," Riley said. "I don't need bad press when I'm asking for a budget increase. Earn your pay!" He reached for his ever-present briefcase and slammed the door behind him.

Several Seattle reporters held their mikes out to Walsh. "Sorry," he said, "we have no further comment at this time." He sidled past them out the door, glad to return to work.

Chapter Seven

Late on a cool, windy Friday afternoon, construction workers, staff members and volunteers posed for photos with DM and her dog. Local press swarmed the area in front of the shelter's office and shouted out questions about the partial reopening.

"I want to thank everyone involved for their great work in getting us back on our feet," DM said. "Particularly, the Seattle kennel company which rushed pre-assembled pieces to an offsite building, where our construction team could work 12-hour days inside. We now have modern touches such as steel, fire-resistant wood and roofs. Also, safety windows and brand-new security cameras added to all structures."

One of the volunteers led the first group of reporters on a tour of the buildings. DM answered more questions from those left behind, thanked everyone again, and headed to the office for hot coffee. She stopped and turned at a tap on her shoulder.

A photographer quickly shot a series of close-up photos using a flash. Temporarily blinded, DM put her out hands and felt the person push her away, causing her to stumble and nearly fall. When her sight cleared, no one was around.

DM shrugged off the incident and was soon inside the small main building, checking in with the front office staff. Ramped up social media postings had caused a flood of interest in adopting the shelter's initial returned group of displaced animals. Soon the rest of the animals would be back at the shelter for their chance to obtain permanent re-homing.

***

Saturday afternoon, Walsh and Laskey attended a Collins Charitable Foundation invitation-only cake and ice cream reception to thank its donors and celebrate the reopening. Caterers set up a special tent with heaters for sixty or so people to comfortably mingle. The guests also enjoyed a chocolate fountain and sundae stations along with several multi-tiered cakes.

Walsh surveyed the crowd and loosened his tie. "I don't like these fancy receptions, but I guess they're necessary."

"It's quite a turnout, boss," Laskey said, sipping fruit punch. "She's got good community support."

He frowned and tossed his paper plate into the trash. "I'd feel better if we were further along in the investigation. The arsonist/killer could be here and we wouldn't even know. Anything new come in before you left the station?"

"No." Laskey made room as DM joined them. "Nice party."

"Thanks." The director looked tired but happy. "We're on our way back, bigger and better. Thank God the public's rallied and given forever homes to so many of our animals. Which reminds me, Detective Walsh," she said with a smile, "how are your cats doing? Do they have you trained yet?"

"Yeah, yeah. I'm at their mercy, which you knew I'd be. They're great company, though." He pulled out his phone and showed off recent photos of the bratty felines.

"He's a proud cat papa," Laskey laughed.

DM met Walsh's eyes and smiled.

Suddenly, Henry, DM's dog, came to full attention in front of her and uttered a low, menacing growl. A short, young, bald man appeared from nowhere and stood at Laskey's elbow. He wore a Cheater's Lake Animal Rescue t-shirt, designer jeans and thin leather jacket.

"Congrats on getting things back to normal, Daisy," he said, lifting his paper cup for a toast. "Remarkable how you manage to claw your way up from the edge of disaster every single time."

He paused. "I'm Tony Kurtz," he told Laskey. "Admired you from afar."

Walsh positioned himself between the women as Laskey shifted away from Kurtz. "How do you know Director Collins?"

Kurtz chuckled. "We grew up together, poor as church mice, back in the hills. Daisy doesn't talk about it in press interviews, but I'm proud of my roots."

DM's dog moved closer to Kurtz, who glared down at the animal and backed away. "Keep control of him, darlin', or he'll have to be put down for viciousness."

"You definitely were not invited." DM raised her voice over the dog's growls. She held tight to Henry's leash as she waved to two of her security team.

Kurtz was escorted out, laughing, aiming his fingers at her in a pretend pistol motion.

"What's the story on the creep? Has he threatened you before?" Walsh made a note of Kurtz's name.

DM sighed. "No, not really. We did grow up together in the same area. Our families hung out but I always found him repulsive. Ever since I left home for Seattle, he turns up everywhere I go, usually asking if I've changed my mind about dating him." She made a disgusted face. "Ugh."

When the reception wound to a close, Walsh and Laskey escorted DM and Henry to her car and followed her home in their marked car.

They were greeted in the driveway by an older couple dressed in dark running clothes. DM introduced them. "Don Santiago worked for my husband and is former military police. His wife, Anne, is a retired FBI agent. They've moved in with Henry and I."

"Daisy is like family to us," Don explained. "After her husband, Ted, died, my wife and I moved to Canada to be near our grandchildren. They are now spread out across the world, so we returned to be with another of our loved ones."

"Glad to hear it," Walsh said, extending his hand and passing each of them his card. "Call me any time if you need our department's assistance or have any leads on what happened at the shelter."

"Thanks, again," DM said, "I appreciate you both coming today. Officer Laskey and I are meeting tomorrow, so I'll see at least one of you again soon." She smiled and entered her house, Don and Anne on each side.

Laskey raised an eyebrow at Walsh.

He shrugged and they returned to the cruiser, headed back to the police station.

Chapter Eight

Sunday dawned warm and sunny for a change. Laskey arrived at DM's home in jeans, boots and a light jacket. DM opened the front door, similarly clad.

"The Santiagos need supplies," DM said, leading Laskey into the kitchen. "I told them you'd be here a couple hours and that we're safe with Henry."

Laskey accepted a bottle of cold water as DM swept a newspaper up from the counter.

"This issue of the Seattle *Times* features a big spread on the shelter. I hope it brings in more families to adopt our animals." DM poured herself a to-go cup of coffee. "Ready to explore?"

The two walked in the woods at the back of the house, Henry off leash and leading the way. Soon they reached a cement pad. "This is the beginning of the area where we'll train rescue dogs for private security and others for therapy," DM said, her red hair brilliant in the sunshine. "There's an incredible need for veterans and others suffering from PTSD and abuse to have trained companions. I also promised dogs for several handicapped children and an organization for the blind. The security training helps subsidize therapy dogs."

"Sounds like a huge undertaking." Laskey inhaled the scent of pine trees and lifted her face to a gentle breeze. "Feels like we might actually have spring."

DM laughed. "Yes, to both. As to the training, I learned a lot from running the prison program. You know about that, don't you?"

"I know you rescued dogs from shelters and matched them with non-violent felons. Then they lived with the prisoners for several months to socialize them."

"Right, following the example I saw at the women's prison that was so successful." DM called to Henry who happily chased a rabbit a short distance from the women. "My dog was a dropout. I couldn't see his being returned to a shelter, though. He and I were too bonded."

"Why'd you name him Henry?" Laskey asked.

"Fond memories of my mother's father, Grampy Henry. He loved all the stray dogs in the mountains other people dumped off to just die. Drove my grandmother Wanda crazy with the swarms of them around the farm." DM chuckled. "Do you have pets, Officer Laskey?"

"Nope, my landlord doesn't allow them. I'm pretty new at the station so my pay doesn't allow for better housing choices."

"I'm curious," DM said. "What made you decide to become a cop?"

Laskey laughed. "I was working in a bar, getting nowhere. Met a couple of Seattle cops passing through and it got me to thinking. I'd managed to get my associate's along the way since high school, so all I had to do was get accepted for training at the academy. Luckily I could pass the physical."

"And then you were hired by Detective Walsh?" DM paused. "I know I'm being nosy, but I don't want to dwell on what happened to Carson and the shelter — at least for one day."

"Detective Walsh agreed to give me a chance."

"So, what's his story? He's obviously very attractive..."

Laskey put her hand out and stopped DM's stride. She pulled her handgun. "There's something off here. The birds stopped their twittering."

DM glanced around. "I don't see anything. I -"

Henry ran toward his owner, barking ferociously. A piece of metal whooshed through the air and an arrow buried deep in the dog's rump. Yelping, he fell to the ground.

Laskey and DM raced to the German Shepherd. DM ran her hands over the dog's body. Laskey pulled out her cell phone but discovered she had no bars.

"No!" DM shouted. "No! I can't lose him. Whoever the hell is out here, you have to get them."

"We will, but right now we've got to carry him to the house and stay together." Laskey removed her jacket and placed it near Henry. "Can you lift?"

Tears streamed down DM's face as she begged Henry not to die. She hefted him onto the jacket, his backend bleeding slightly with the embedded arrow. The women slowly made their way back to the house, pulling the dog carefully over the forest floor. Laskey continuously scanned the area, her weapon ready.

***

Walsh arrived a few minutes after Laskey's call for back-up. She met him on the front porch, updating him on the attack.

"The shelter's vet drove over from his home close to here and stabilized Henry. The Santiagos returned from errands in Seattle and they've all headed to the vet's emergency clinic."

"Good. Show me the place where the dog got hit." Walsh motioned two patrol officers who had just arrived to follow them. "One of you to the right, one to the left. Circle around and meet us back here unless you find something. It's gonna be hard to track on the muddy paths but use the whistle if you see anything that resembles an arrow."

When Laskey knelt on the ground to show Walsh Henry's blood, they heard a whistle.

"Detective," one of them said as Walsh and Laskey approached, "we found a bandana with blood on it near the path out of here." He showed the blue cloth encased in a plastic bag. "That's it, though."

"Great work, it's something." Walsh took the bag and told the men they could return to the station. He and Laskey did another circle and returned to DM's house.

Walsh sat on a porch swing beside Laskey. "I don't like that someone got this close to DM and tried to take out her dog. The perp had to know the Santiagos weren't here."

"Should we start with Kurtz?" Laskey asked. "He seemed to hate the dog and has history with DM."

"Yeah, and recheck the disgruntled prison participants, too. We must have missed something. I don't buy that everyone's clean and all alibied. This feels personal and like it's ramping up."

A little while later, DM finally returned with the Santiagos and without Henry. "He didn't require surgery, but he's sedated, on IV's and staying overnight," she told them. "Doc says he'll be okay, after some time to recuperate, no permanent damage, thank God."

"We found a bandana with blood on it out in the woods." Walsh showed it to her. "Do you recognize it?"

DM rubbed her eyes. "No. I'll let you know how Henry's doing. Tomorrow's my day to be in the office at the shelter." She yawned and shuffled into the house.

Walsh watched her close the door and flip the porch light on.

Don Santiago leaned against a post on the porch stairs. "Seems like a warning to me. I think she's the target. We'll try to convince her to relocate to a place with less access, maybe her condo in Seattle."

Walsh nodded. "Keep in touch. In the meantime, I'll have a patrol swing by each shift. Glad you're here."

He and Laskey reversed their vehicles around the driveway and headed for the police station.

***

Back at the department, Laskey plunked herself down at her desk and frowned at a big pile of paperwork. She'd just started to attack the mess when Shawn, the department's clerk, came in with a cup of coffee and plate of cookies. He was short and slight, and teased mercilessly around the station for always wearing a shirt and tie.

"You need sugar," he said, also handing her some message slips. "There's a few calls into Crime Stoppers the chief wants you to review."

She put the slips near her phone. "Anything else happening?"

"The boss is in with the chief getting his butt chewed for lack of progress on the Collins' case. There's another press conference next week and the department's not looking good."

Laskey rolled her eyes. "Thanks."

Shawn took some papers from her out-basket and left for his office.

Walsh joined her an hour later, taking a call on his cell as he lowered himself into her visitor chair. "Wait a minute," he said into the phone. "Someone recognized Carson Butts from the newspaper article?" Walsh paused to listen. "Who the hell is he?" Another pause. "No way."

He ended the call and took a cookie from Laskey's plate, eating it in two bites. "Carson Butts had an interesting previous life before he hitched his star to DM Collins. Turns out, he was an accountant for a crime family in Chicago. When the Feds moved in to close things down, Butts, actual name Clarence Branson, disappeared. He left behind a wife and kids."

"Who called this in?" Laskey asked, her laptop open and running a Google search.

Walsh laughed. "His wife. She's a notary public and in Seattle for a convention. Dialed the FBI immediately."

"Amazing. So, do they take over the case?"

Before Walsh could answer, the chief stopped in the doorway. "Feds want this department to keep going on Butts/Branson, whatever his name is. Be real nice if you could find *something* about the murder and arson, Walsh, and soon. We, as usual, look like idiots and the *Times* article doesn't help our image." He stomped away down the hallway, cursing.

"Great," Walsh sighed. "Any luck on Kurtz?"

"I sent patrol over to his penthouse. No one's home. The doorman said Kurtz hasn't been around since Saturday night and neither has his girlfriend." Laskey stretched her arms over her head. "Girlfriend's a photographer, Caroline Morris. Shawn's checking out her details."

"You've been at it all day, Laskey. Go home. We'll hit it fresh and hard in the morning." Walsh banged his knee on the corner of her desk. "Dammit. See you tomorrow."

Laskey grabbed her cold coffee and jacket. She grinned at Walsh. "DM's sweet on you, you know."

Walsh crumpled a piece of paper and threw it at her head. "I told you to get outta here."

"Yeah, yeah," she laughed and shut the door behind her.

Chapter Nine

DM Collins paced around the Cheaters Lake Police Department conference room. Painted gray, it was dark and gloomy, mirroring the spring afternoon. She'd been cooling her heels a half hour for Detective Walsh, after his call asking her to come into the station. The only person she'd seen at all was a clerk named Shawn, who offered coffee and apologies for the delay. With a sigh, she checked her watch again and mentally ran down the list of things she needed to do as the day wasted away.

Finally, Walsh entered and motioned her to take a seat. "Sorry to keep you waiting. We've had a couple of developments," Coatless, tie undone and shirtsleeves rolled up. His piercing blue eyes were bloodshot but focused intently on her green ones.

"D-developments?" DM stuttered at his full-on attention. "You know who killed Carson?"

"Not yet. We've been trying to locate your friend, Tony Kurtz, and a photographer, Caroline Morris." He set photos of three people on the table along with a gray folder.

DM glanced at the glossy enlargements and touched his forearm. "Wait. I've seen that woman before. She's always taking pictures of me, at every press event and some of the parties I've hosted. Is she connected to Kurtz?"

Walsh shrugged. "Doorman at Kurtz's place says she's his girlfriend. Both have disappeared. But another possible player was arrested this morning. A con named Art —"

"— Bezzo." She interrupted him again, holding a photograph. "He was at the prison when I ran the dog training program there. He applied for a spot but I turned him down. Something about him made me cautious. I didn't get the feeling he liked animals any more than humans —just wanted some points to get an earlier release."

"We ran prints on the bloody bandana found at your place close to where Henry was shot. Bezzo popped up in the system. Before he demanded a lawyer, he admitted he works for Kurtz."

"Tony's behind this?" She shook her head. "I can't believe he'd go that far." She pushed her chair away and moved over to a window, watching raindrops hit the glass, a bleak parking lot outside.

"We'll charge Bezzo with trespassing and wounding your dog, but we don't have evidence he started the fire or killed Carson. Do you remember anything else about him from the prison program?" Walsh rose from his chair, stretched and joined DM at the window.

She looked up at him, eyes filled with tears. "Why would they do any of this? How could they hate me so much?"

"Trying to understand how people like this think will drive you crazy. There's more." He gave her his handkerchief.

Once they both were again seated, Walsh tapped his file folder. "Your Carson Butts was living a double life. His real name is Clarence Branson. He was a mob accountant from Chicago. Walked away from that life when the Feds were closing in. His wife identified him from the *Times* article about the shelter."

DM dabbed tears on her cheeks. "He lied to me, too?"

Walsh cleared his throat. "Probably desperate when he stumbled into your shelter construction site. You said he was good with the animals. Maybe he was trying to atone for his sins." Walsh paused. "You okay?"

DM straightened her spine. "I'm fine. Henry's coming home tomorrow and we'll get back to normal. If you have more questions, let's just do this and get it over with."

"Okay. I understand the shelter contracts out for vet services. Do you have any kind of clinic for onsite treatment?" Walsh ran his hand through his hair as he waited for her reply.

"We have first aid equipment for humans and a couple of drugs for the animals. The vials are kept in a locked cabinet." DM rubbed her eyes. "Only C-Carson and I have keys..."

"Do you know how much Ketamine you keep on hand?"

"No, but not too much. I think every animal shelter stocks it to calm hurt animals. Why are you asking about that drug?" She met Walsh's penetrating gaze.

"I'm sorry, DM," Walsh said, "but Carson was injected with it and his heart stopped. He was dead before the fire."

Her body shook. She wept so hard, she couldn't catch her breath. Walsh moved around the chairs and knelt next to her, taking one of her hands. "It'll be all right," he said.

She felt the warmth of his large hand and a stirring in her heart. He was the nicest man she'd met since her husband, but this was not the time for romantic thoughts.

"I don't think it'll ever be okay again." DM drew a raspy breath.

Walsh reached under the table and pressed a button, then stood and moved away from her, positioning himself near the door.

A couple of minutes later, Laskey came in with tissues and water. While she saw to DM, Walsh pulled out his cell phone and spoke in a low voice.

"I've called Don and Anne to get you," Walsh told DM. "We'll talk again later."

***

After DM left, Walsh returned to his office. He sipped hot tea from the mug on his desk and punched Greg's number into his phone. His friend answered on the first ring.

"Hogan's Chinese."

"Real cute," Walsh said. "Got anything for me on Butts and Kurtz?"

Greg tapped a few keys on his computer. "Butts was in the clear till a few months ago. Someone at the FBI decided to look into cold cases involving the Chicago mob and his disappearance popped up."

"Hmm..." Walsh doodled on his pad of paper. "Was there a reward for him?"

"Not that I could find. It would take some digging to even know about it outside the agency, but I think that's where your Kurtz fits in." Greg paused. "Ready for more?"

"Sure." Walsh sighed. "Been a great day so far, lay it on me."

"Tony Kurtz grew up near your DM Collins, like they both said. He relocated to Seattle after the lady and hovered around as she got herself an education and a rich husband. Kurtz eventually ended up publisher and writer for an alternative arts magazine. As a journalist, he's got fingers in a lot of pies and access to info out the ying-yang."

Walsh yawned and apologized. "Do tell."

"Kurtz featured DM in the magazine a couple of times, mostly her charity and animal interests. He slants the stuff to make Ms. Collins look like an opportunist. I emailed the links to you."

"So, exactly how'd Kurtz go from broke backcountry hillbilly to heading up a sleek artsy magazine?" Walsh made a face at his watery tea and pushed the mug aside. "Win the lottery?"

"Petty crimes at first," Greg said, "and he's got a record using three aliases. Then he glommed on to a patron of the arts he charmed at one of Collins' shindigs, before, of course, they booted his uninvited ass out."

"Crimes involving violence?" Walsh asked.

"Nope, paper stuff like bounced checks, some fraud. He was living hand to mouth for a few years and cutting some corners. I've emailed Shawn that data, too."

"Where's the patron of the arts these days?"

"Her name's Sandy Morris-Leyton. Very particular about the hyphen. She's the one who gave Kurtz the magazine. It was a pet project of hers but losing money. She dropped loser Kurtz in time to start up with a politician. Hubby Lee Leyton ran for Seattle City Council and is currently serving his successful second term."

Walsh flipped through a pile of paperwork. "Does she have a daughter, Caroline?"

"Hold on."

While he waited for Greg to check, Walsh buzzed Laskey.

"Yep. Daughter Caroline. You know her?"

"Maybe. I'll call you back. Thanks, Greg."

Chapter Ten

Sharon Laskey carefully placed her nearly full wineglass on the thick white tablecloth and smiled at the man sitting across from her. Jeremy, body-to-die-for, the personal trainer from her gym. With its soft music and candlelit tables, the Seattle restaurant was her favorite for a romantic date.

"A man could get lost in those pretty brown eyes, Sharon," he leaned in and whispered. "Come back to my place tonight."

"I'll have to leave early for work, like last time," she smiled. "Can you handle that?"

Jeremy laughed and took her hand. "Let's go. I'll be glad to show you what I can 'handle'."

They stepped out of the warm Italian restaurant and into the dry, inky black Seattle night. He held the sports car door open as his date slid inside. Before he got to the driver's side, her cell phone rang. She looked at the caller ID, swore to herself and answered the call.

"Sorry to call so late," Walsh said. "The department's short-handed here with a road rage incident and multi-vehicle crash. I need you at Seattle General Hospital ER as soon as possible on the Collins' matter."

"I'm in Seattle already." Sharon covered the phone and sighed. Then, addressing both men, she said, "I'll be at the hospital in ten minutes."

Her one night off in months, a third date with the ultra-sexy trainer, and, of course, she was called into work. Good thing she'd had only a swallow of the wine.

***

"Cheater's Lake Police Officer Sharon Laskey." She offered her badge to a hospital security guard. "Seattle PD called about a gunshot wound admitted to the ER."

The guard nodded and pointed down a long hallway. "Treatment Area B-6 at the end. Your guy will be transferred upstairs to a room soon. PD's waiting for you."

Laskey swore under her breath as she moved along the endless hallway. Dressed in a too-tight little black dress and high heels, there was no time to change. So much for a professional appearance.

In the curtained alcove, two SPD officers stood near the foot of a patient's bed. The younger man whistled when Laskey introduced herself. "If that's a new trend in uniforms, I like it," he said, eyebrows wriggling.

She ignored him.

"Shut up," the older one rolled his eyes. "Officer Laskey, we got your BOLO on Kurtz here. Someone shot him in the leg and pushed him out of a car in front of the ER entrance."

Laskey looked over Kurtz. He was handcuffed to the bedrails, eyes closed, seemingly asleep. A bulky bandage covered his upper thigh and specks of blood dotted his naked chest.

Kurtz stirred and peered up at Laskey. "Hey, I know you! It's your job to get that bitch who shot me."

"Mr. Kurtz," Laskey said in her reasonable tone, "let's start at the beginning."

"She tried to kill me!" Kurtz yelled. "What are you and the rest of your lousy cop buddies going to do about it?"

Laskey pulled a chair up to the bed. "Start at the beginning. Where were you this evening?"

Kurtz glared at her and his voice rose again. "Okay, I'll play your game. In the parking garage at my condo. I was taking a box out of my trunk when I felt something tear into me. I didn't realize then it was a bullet. I fell and hit my head. There's gotta be video. She did it and I want her arrested!"

"You got a good look at the shooter?"

"Yeah, a woman. Daisy Marigold Collins. Go arrest her." He struggled to catch his breath. "She's wanted to kill me for years and finally got her chance."

"Were there any other witnesses?"

"No! I told you, I was in the parking garage, not in a Macy's." Kurtz shook his head. "You aren't listening to me."

"What about your girlfriend, Caroline Morris? Was she with you tonight?" Laskey asked.

"I dumped Morris' ass two days ago. I was alone. I know it was Daisy, but of course you don't believe me. Cheater's Lake PD is on her side because she's bought you off." Kurtz pulled at his handcuffs and rattled the bed.

The SPD officers grabbed his hands. "Cut it out," the older one said. "You aren't going anywhere."

Kurtz pretended to calm down, took a deep breath, and screamed for a nurse. "Cops are beating me! Help! Somebody help me!"

***

Back in Cheater's Lake, Laskey checked the time on the dashboard clock in Walsh's cruiser. Four o'clock in the morning. She sipped at a large, black coffee and waited for Walsh to return to his car. The accident/crime scene finally cleared, she watched as her boss processed the release of everyone and sent them home for some sleep.

"God, it's been endless," Walsh said with a yawn, getting behind the wheel. "Lucky no one was killed in the chase and the crashes, but we have two critical, including a five-year old. Absolutely stupid waste."

"I'm sorry I wasn't around to help," Laskey said.

"Forget it. You deserved a night off, but that kinda got wrecked, too. What happened with Kurtz?" He stopped the car at a red light.

She stifled a yawn. "Arrested for being combative. Taken to SPD's hospital jail and admitted overnight. The gunshot was a through and through, should have been simple, but he was out of control. He claims DM Collins shot him."

"What?" Walsh gave her his full attention. "What? He said DM did it?" Could he have been that wrong about her?

A car beeped its horn behind them. Walsh flipped on his light bar, reached out the window and waved the vehicle around them.

"Yup. The chief put out a BOLO on her. She's nowhere to be found, and neither are Don and Anne Santiago. The dog's not at the vet, either."

"Just when it can't get any worse. This doesn't sound right." Walsh shook his head.

"You don't think she's capable of shooting someone who's been stalking her for years?"

Walsh drew up to Laskey's apartment complex. "I'm too tired to think. Come back in at noon and we'll deal with it all."

"Okay, thanks for the ride."

"Laskey, one more thing." Walsh leaned over toward her as she got out. "You look nice."

She smiled and watched him drive away.

Chapter Eleven

Two days later, Detective Walsh and Officer Laskey took their seats across from DM Collins in Interrogation Room No. 1 of the Cheater's Lake police station. Laskey raised an eyebrow at him, but he shook his head. He'd play bad cop and get to the bottom of this.

DM twisted her hands and gazed down at the metal table.

"DM Collins, you have waived counsel and agreed to be interviewed under oath regarding the shooting of Tony Kurtz. This session is being videotaped. Your statements will be transcribed in written form for your review and signature. Do you understand?" Walsh asked.

She murmured "Yes."

"Sorry," Laskey said. "You have to speak up for the microphone."

"Yes, Detective Walsh," DM said, lifting her chin to meet his hard eyes. "I understand."

"Let's begin," Walsh said and pushed the record button. "You came into the station two days ago, at my request, to answer some questions regarding events that occurred at your animal rescue shelter. Is that correct?"

"Yes."

"Tell me where you went after you left our conference room that afternoon."

DM hesitated.

"Ms. Collins —"

"Don and Anne Santiago picked me up in their SUV and at my insistence, took me to the vet's to get Henry, even though it was a day early for him to come home. I couldn't stand another night without him. We were headed back to my house in Cheater's Lake when a very large, dark pickup tried to run us off the road." DM paused and sipped from a bottled water.

"We managed to outrun him and get away. Since it didn't seem safe to go home, Don drove into Seattle. He stopped the SUV at a traffic light near my condo and we were rammed in the rear by the same truck."

"Did you report this to the police?" Walsh asked.

"No." DM picked at the label on her bottle. "Don got us out of there and over the water to Bellevue. He pulled into a shopping center, then found a tracker under the car and removed it, tossing it into a trashcan. We drove to his friend's auto repair garage and left the SUV, borrowed a beat up old Subaru. Finally, we ended up in Tacoma at Anne's cousin's. He hid us in his house, while Don made calls to some retired military friends about the pickup and the tracker."

Walsh stopped the tape and reviewed a page of notes. He pushed the button to restart. "We'll need the names and addresses of everywhere you went, everyone you saw, unless you're prepared to give them to us now."

"N-no. Don and Anne will know." She bit her lower lip.

"They'll also be interviewed. Let's continue. What happened next?"

"We spent the night in Tacoma. In the morning, we were eating breakfast and saw the news on TV about Tony being shot. I figured maybe Art Bezzo got bailed out and went after him." DM sighed. "Perhaps that was wishful thinking."

Laskey noted herself for the tape. "Ms. Collins, Tony Kurtz positively identified you as his shooter. How can you explain that?"

DM shook her head. "How could I shoot him when I wasn't even around?"

The Interrogation Room door opened. Chief Riley motioned Walsh out.

***

Walsh returned, put them back on the record and glared at DM. "Do you know what the penalty is for obstructing an active police investigation?"

"W-what?" DM stuttered. "I'm not obstructing. I've told you the truth." Her face paled and eyes filled with tears. "You have to believe me."

"You can save the waterworks. This camera says otherwise." He pointed to a screen. The three of them watched a video taken outside the Seattle General Hospital's ER entrance. "Who's the redhead, Ms. Collins? The one struggling to pull Kurtz out of the car registered to you?"

DM buried her head in her hands and sobbed. "I didn't do it. Someone was trying to kill me." After a few moments, she lifted herself back up against the hard chair. "I want a lawyer."

"Interview ended," Walsh said. He gathered his notes and slammed out of the room.

Laskey handed DM tissues. "An officer will get you a phone to call your lawyer." She shut the door quietly behind her.

***

An hour later, Walsh stood behind Chief Riley when he called the press conference to order. "Cheater's Lake Police announce today that

Ms. DM Collins, director of the Cheater's Lake Animal Rescue Shelter, has been arrested and charged with the attempted murder of Tony Kurtz, of Seattle. Mr. Kurtz is the publisher of ARTSY Magazine. He remains hospitalized in good condition with a gunshot wound to his leg." He nodded to Walsh.

"The investigation is continuing," Walsh said. He left without answering any questions.

***

At home, Walsh hung up his suit jacket, pulled off the hated tie, kicked off his shoes and spread out on his living room sectional. The couch and TV were the only furniture in his construction zone of a house. He was still in the middle of replacing old carpeting with new hardwood floors throughout the place in his spare time. His very rare spare time.

Walsh ate barbeque takeout and mindlessly watched a basketball game. Fred and Ethel hovered nearby, occasionally rewarded with bits of meat in a small dish their human set on the floor for them. He was in the kitchen for more beer when his cell rang and he recognized the caller.

"Greg," he growled.

"Hey, Markie, how's it hanging up there in the rainstorms? You sound grumpy."

"It's the Collins' case driving me nuts. Find anything new for me? We aren't getting anywhere after the chief pushed to have her charged with attempted murder." Walsh took a big swig of cold beer.

"Nothing yet on that score. I was thinking of coming for a visit in a couple weeks, though. You receiving company?" Greg asked.

"You're not company. Hurry and get here. I don't have anyone else to tell me the facts of life and offer unending, unsolicited advice."

Greg laughed. "We've all been taken in by a beautiful woman, Markie."

"Who said anything about —never mind. I was taken in. She's a gorgeous woman who I thought could tell the truth. Joke's on me."

"What have you got on her for attempted murder?"

Walsh explained Kurtz's statement, the videos and Collins' unproven alibi.

"Just a thought but couldn't someone else be impersonating Ms. Collins? And if she, or whoever, wanted to kill Kurtz, why a shot to the leg?"

The two friends spoke a little longer. Walsh finished his meal, showered and went to bed. He tossed and turned through most of the night, replaying the Collins' case and Greg's questions.

Chapter Twelve

Early the next morning, Officer Sharon Laskey knocked on Detective Walsh's office door and entered without waiting for his reply. She handed him a large herbal tea and pushed aside a pile of folders to sit on his visitor's chair. "You doing okay?"

"Of course. Why wouldn't I be?" he snapped.

"Because you like DM and you believed her, at least at first."

Yeah, he'd believed her. Just like he'd bought his ex-wife's stories till he caught her in bed with his "superior" officer, back in Phoenix.

"She's lawyered up." Walsh motioned for her to start. "Let's review what we have so far."

"Cameras in the garage recorded a redhead driving a Lexus and parking it two rows from Kurtz's BMW. He's struggling to pull a box of gym equipment out of his trunk and turns his head toward a noise. Then he's shot in the leg and falls to the concrete. The redhead's car drives back to the BMW, facing away from the camera. A few minutes later, she rips out of the parking garage with lights off. We don't have any further traffic cams as yet."

Walsh sipped some tea. "Thanks for this. Sorry to be so rude."

Laskey smiled. "Kurtz has been released from the hospital, so I guess that's the good news. Bad news—Don and Anne Santiago have also lawyered up. I've been trying without their input to track down the details of the truck that chased them, the Bellevue shopping center trash cans where the tracker was allegedly tossed, auto repair shop and the Subaru, and, of course, Anne's cousin in Tacoma who let them stay the night."

"And?"

"Shawn's got a tech guy looking at footage from the Seattle street camera near DM's condo. There's a partial plate on the pickup. That's about it, so far."

"So, there was a pickup? Great." A point for DM. Maybe he'd been too quick to judge her?

"I did stop by the vet's office on my way in. Since he recognized me from the dog's shooting, he told me Henry should've stayed another day, but DM insisted on his release." Laskey opened her coffee. "It's not much, but it matches DM's statement about that detail."

"Yeah. How about this for a theory—what if the redhead who shot Kurtz wasn't DM? When Greg and I talked about it last night, he also wondered why the shooter only shot Kurtz in the leg if she really wanted to kill him." Walsh paused. "What do you think?"

Laskey nodded. "Interesting. Do we have proof that DM has a gun and knows how to use it? Too bad it was too late to test her for gunshot residue...also weird there was only one shot. Seems to me if a woman wants to hurt a guy that bad, she'd fire a couple of times."

Walsh doodled on a pad near his phone.

"Boss, I've wondered if maybe DM, or whoever, had help getting Kurtz in and out of the car. She's a lot smaller than he is."

"No one else is shown on the videos, though."

"I know," Laskey nodded, "but an angry felon like Art Bezzo, for example, might have enough experience to avoid cameras."

"Good thinking." Walsh nodded. "Check with Shawn and see if Bezzo's out of jail."

***

Walsh looked up when Chief Riley entered his office and plopped onto the edge of the desk. "Good, you're both just sitting around. You're the first to hear DM Collins has been cut loose."

"Out on bail?" Walsh asked.

"No, unfortunately. The charges have been dismissed." Riley snorted. "Pays to hire the top lawyers in the country. Our prosecutor folded."

Walsh was momentarily speechless. "She was telling the truth, after all."

"What happened, Chief?" Laskey asked.

"Don Santiago brought in proof of her alibi. Now we have to find out who really tried to kill that scum, Kurtz. Of course, the original arson and murder cases haven't even been solved. So, it's still all yours, Walsh. I expect you to jump on it." Riley stalked out of the office.

"Has the Fire Marshal been able to connect Art Bezzo to the arson yet?" Walsh tossed a pile of folders into his out-box.

"No," Laskey frowned, "but we should ask him more questions about Kurtz. That seems to set him off. He's out on bail."

"Let's locate the elusive Caroline Morris, Kurtz's *alleged* girlfriend." Walsh grabbed his raincoat. "If we can first get to the cruiser without drowning in this storm."

***

As Walsh drove, Laskey scrolled down her phone. Caroline Morris' Facebook page offered her schedule for the day— photographing an anchor at a downtown Seattle TV station for a national magazine. Laskey was constantly amazed people would advertise to thieves in the area that they weren't home.

"You handle Morris," Walsh said, "and I'll drag Bezzo back to the station for questioning about Kurtz's shooting. Take the lady in if she's not cooperative." He stopped the car in front of a downtown skyscraper. "Call me if you need backup."

Laskey pulled up the hood of her jacket and fought the rain and wind to the building's entrance. After a short chat with the security guard, she was escorted to the penthouse suite and the photo session.

A break was called just as Laskey entered the studio. She approached the photographer. "Ms. Morris?"

"I'm working. Whatever you're selling will have to wait." Morris ignored her and roughly moved two pieces of lighting equipment a few inches. She yelled to an intern to "get off your ass" and "pay attention."

The young man rolled his eyes behind her back.

"When I saw your Facebook post, I thought you'd be modeling with the anchor."

Morris looked at Laskey and laughed. "He's gay. I can do better."

"Like Tony Kurtz?"

Her face darkened. "Who the hell are you? How'd you get on this set? Security! I need Security!"

Laskey identified herself and showed her badge. "We can take this conversation down to the station right now, Ms. Morris. Your choice."

"I'm not going anywhere with you. That badge looks like it came from a cereal box." She jabbed her finger into Laskey's chest. "Back off, bitch."

Laskey grabbed Morris' hand, whipped it around her back and handcuffed her. "Assault on a police officer is a serious crime, Miss Morris. These security people are witnesses." She called Walsh for backup.

Morris swore and tried to fight being hustled to a patrol car by two officers. No one offered to help defend her honor or assist her in an escape. Several people laughed and took photos with their cellphones, probably then posted them on social media with various comments.

***

In the police station's Interrogation Room No. 1, Walsh explained to Art Bezzo that he'd be asked questions under oath and the session would be recorded.

"The AC's not working, Mr. Bezzo," Walsh began, "I apologize it's like a sauna in here, but maybe we'll get the door opened. While we're waiting for maintenance, let's discuss the shooting of Tony Kurtz."

"I ain't saying nothing. I told you I want a lawyer." Bezzo glared at him.

Someone knocked on the door.

"Detective Walsh," Shawn said, entering the room, "I'm sorry to interrupt, but Officer Laskey is here with Caroline Morris."

Walsh nodded. Shawn left the interrogation room door open as he went back out into the hallway.

"Morris?" Art Bezzo bellowed, shifting in his chair. "What's she doing here?"

Laskey hesitated for a moment in front of the doorway, the handcuffed Morris still squawking and complaining as they stopped.

"Wait a minute!" Morris yelled. "What's Art-the-Arsonist doing here?"

"What did you call him?" Laskey asked.

"No way he's ratting me out. I'll tell you what really happened with Tony Kurtz. Art shot him, not me." Morris attempted to kick Laskey. "Take these cuffs off and I'll tell you everything."

Bezzo partly jerked from his chair, but his cuffed hands held him to the table. "You're not getting away with it, you little bitch. No wonder Kurtz dumped you. He shoulda shut you up for good. You and your stupid little pictures."

Walsh held up two fingers and Laskey smiled. "We're going to Interrogation Room No. 2, Ms. Morris."

An hour later, Walsh and Laskey met to compare notes.

***

At his desk, Walsh opened two bottles of water and gave one to Laskey. "Shall we toast?"

Laskey laughed. "What a couple of winners. Why don't you go first?"

"Art-the-Arsonist Bezzo waived a lawyer for possible charges in the shooting of Tony Kurtz. He claims Morris offered him money to come with her, but she did the shooting. He was merely there to help if she needed it. He only dragged Kurtz's body in and out of the car so Kurtz could get medical care."

"But we don't have him on tape doing that," Laskey said.

"I told him we had two videos. He was so busy falling all over himself implicating Morris, he didn't follow up." Walsh laughed. "Sloppy."

"What about the arson?"

"That," Walsh said, "he won't cop to. What'd you get from Morris?"

Laskey shook her head. "She's a piece of work. Cried non-stop but managed to waive an attorney, also. Told me she was sure as a woman, I'd understand that Kurtz used and abused her. She just couldn't think straight. On a whim, she 'borrowed' DM's car from her condo garage, put on a red wig, and drove back to Tony's to scare him."

"Uh huh. And hired Art to help her, why?"

"Because," Laskey rolled her eyes, "she was afraid Tony might try to hurt her again. She wanted his attention, for him to love her, instead of DM. But there's something else—she offered to roll over on Bezzo for a reduced sentence. Claims she has phone recordings of Kurtz hiring Bezzo for the arson of DM's animal shelter."

Walsh smiled. "I know it's not Christmas yet, but it seems like Santa about broke his back with all these great gifts. Nice job, Officer Laskey."

Laskey tapped her water bottle with his. "Thanks, Boss."

"It's finally stopped raining," Walsh said. "Let's go pay Tony Kurtz a visit. He should be able to answer questions after his rest from a mild concussion and leg wound."

Chapter Thirteen

Walsh stood next to Laskey outside the Seattle condo. At Laskey's knock, a gray-haired woman opened the door to the opulent digs and motioned the two inside. "I'm Mr. Kurtz's housekeeper, Marta. He's resting on the couch but is expecting you. Please follow me."

Tony Kurtz sprawled over the sofa with his leg propped on pillows and glared at Walsh and Laskey as they entered the living room. He pointed a remote and muted the sound of a reality show blaring from the massive TV screen. "What do you want? Here to apologize for letting Daisy go after she tried to kill me?"

Walsh glanced around the room and at the floor-to-ceiling windows. He and Laskey removed their coats and sat on another couch opposite Kurtz's.

"Mr. Kurtz," Walsh said, "DM Collins has a rock-solid alibi for the time you were shot. Do you know anyone else who'd want to harm you?"

"*I'm* supposed to solve the crime? Why don't you dazzle me and figure it out." Kurtz winced as he moved back against the cushions.

"We've arrested two of your associates, but both accuse the other of shooting you." Walsh smiled. "Want to guess who they are?"

"I don't have any 'associates'. You're bluffing, Walsh."

Laskey placed photos of Caroline Morris and Art Bezzo on the coffee table between the couches and slid them closer to Kurtz. "Do these people look familiar?" she asked.

Kurtz glanced at the pictures and frowned. "No idea."

Walsh laughed. "Don't even know your own girlfriend?"

"Mr. Kurtz," Laskey stood and pulled a set of handcuffs from her belt, "you are under arrest for conspiracy to commit arson. You have the right to remain silent—"

Kurtz leapt from the couch and promptly fell on the carpet, screaming in pain. "Marta, call Security! Then call my lawyer!"

Ignoring his tirade, Laskey continued *Mirandizing* him, while Walsh pulled Kurtz up and into his wheelchair tucked beside the TV.

"Art's a convicted felon!" Kurtz yelled. "Morris is a grifter like her mother. You're never gonna make this charge stick. I'll sue you and your department for every goddamn dime you have."

Within a few minutes, the still protesting Kurtz was seat-belted into the back of the police cruiser and headed for Cheater's Lake.

* * *

Chief Riley waited in the lobby of the Cheater's Lake Police station and shook his head as he watched Walsh and Laskey arrive, book Kurtz, and bundle him down the open hallway to a cell. When they returned and closed the door to Kurtz's yelling, Riley pointed to his office.

"You two are quite the pair," Riley said, seated at his desk while they stood. "Walsh, the hotshot homicide dick transferred from the booming metropolis of Phoenix, Arizona, to sleepy little Cheater's Lake. And Laskey, a former barmaid turned wannabe cop. Unbelievable. You've arrested the *victim* of a crime. What kind of policing do you two call that?"

"Sir," Walsh said through a mostly clenched jaw, "we have evidence that Tony Kurtz hired Art Bezzo to set fire to the animal shelter. We also can prove that Bezzo tried to kill Ms. Collins' dog and narrowly missed her with his crossbow. And we know that Caroline Morris shot Kurtz as part of a lovers' quarrel."

"Fascinating. Do go on." Riley smirked. "I'm waiting to hear who killed the caretaker—Butts, Branson, whatever his name. You've been spending time on the small fish. Who's the real murderer?"

"We're still investigating," Walsh said.

"Yeah, Detective, the same line you throw out at every press conference. It doesn't impress me. Solve the murder before the FBI takes the Branson case back and makes us look even more bumbling than we already do. Both of you get out of here and do your jobs. That is all." Riley waved them away and picked up his phone to make a call.

Chapter Fourteen

Early on Saturday morning, DM lifted her face to the sun and breathed a sigh of relief. "It's a gorgeous day, Henry," she patted her dog, "and perfect for the big event we have planned." The German Shepherd gazed up at her and made quick work of the small biscuit she offered. With the rain finally stopped, warm sunshine bathed the site of the Cheater's Lake Animal Rescue and a small breeze dispersed the scent of rich soil and freshly mown grass.

She checked in first at the office where three volunteers organized piles of handouts, along with plates of donuts and urns of coffee, tea and cider. The clean white walls and counters sparkled, offset with a variety of fresh cut flowers spread about the room. A banner over the door proclaimed, *Low-Cost Spay and Neuter, Free Microchipping, 9 AM Today.*

In the driveway, a stream of people and their pets had lined up more than an hour before the opening time. The crowd talked and joked as they waited for the bargain services.

Detective Mark Walsh, freshly shaved and sporting sunglasses, wore jeans and a Phoenix Suns sweatshirt. He stood far back in line, a cat carrier on each side of him.

DM, with Henry close by, walked among the gathering, greeting everyone and posing for selfies when asked. She reached Walsh's spot and nodded. "Good morning, Detective."

"Good morning." Walsh smiled. "As you can see, I've brought Fred and Ethel. I'm a very responsible pet owner. How are you doing? I was wondering if —"

"As well as anyone falsely accused of a crime." She nodded again and moved on past him down the driveway. He might look delicious, but she wasn't buying the charm today.

Walsh sighed. The woman was obviously very pissed and not receptive to anything he had to say. He didn't blame her, but he was only doing his job. He watched for a while as she continued welcoming pet owners, the sound of her laughter wafting in the air. For him, no laugh, no warmth.

He turned back around to see a large man in a black jacket and pulled down baseball cap slide into line behind him. He wasn't accompanied by any animal.

Walsh heard the click of a lighter a few times, then saw a large plume of smoke from the guy's exhale. During the next couple of minutes, the man steadily tapped his nails against the lighter.

Just as Walsh moved around to comment on the tapping, Fred and Ethel stirred in their carriers. Each hissed and spit, attempting to reach through the bars and claw the nearest humans. "What's the matter with you guys?" Walsh knelt down to their level. "Cut it out."

Black jacket guy swore under his breath and stepped aside, allowing the last half dozen people to move up. He spun away toward the office.

A volunteer came through the line with paperwork for the pet owners and Walsh's attention was diverted to the task at hand.

The bigger tented clinic area opened promptly a few minutes later. One of the technicians announced no animals would be hospitalized after their procedures unless medically necessary. She explained pets would be fine at home as long as they were kept warm and checked on during the night. Three local vets then performed permanent birth control, one animal after another, in the assembly line they'd set up. At the same time, a smaller tent housed a vet and technician efficiently injecting microchips.

While Fred and Ethel underwent their surgeries, Walsh picked up tea and a donut from the office. In a corner of the lobby, DM supervised photos of Henry posing with other pets as part of the shelter's annual fundraiser. He thought about approaching DM when she finished but figured it for a bad idea. Instead, he walked to his car and punched Laskey's number on his cell.

"Morning, Boss."

"I'm at the animal shelter getting the cats fixed. Anything new?" Walsh asked as he leaned against the vehicle. He made a mental note to get his cruiser washed on the way home.

"Nope. No leads on Branson. Everything's quiet. How's DM?"

Walsh ignored Laskey's question. "I'll check in later." He stopped brushing car dust from his pants when he heard DM's screams.

Outside the office building, the strange man previously behind him in line used his large arm around DM's neck to drag her away.

Walsh pulled his weapon and shouted for him to stop. His phone fell to the ground as he ran to catch up with them. The two quickly disappeared in back of the kennels, the only direction to go toward the woods.

***

DM fought against her assailant, a foot taller and easily a hundred pounds heavier. He gripped her so hard she saw stars. She tried to pitch forward to stop their progress. That move ended when he flipped her around, then hit her with a vicious backhand slap which made her ears ring and eyes water.

"You helped destroy my life, you bitch!" The man yelled into her face. "All uppity with your husband's money while the rest of us starved. You didn't care then, but you will now. Forget about your precious dog and your stupid animal rescue. No one's gonna rescue you, baby doll. No one." He swept DM off her feet and carried her upside down over his shoulder and back. His steady progress over the twisted, muddy path, deeper into the woods, left Walsh too far behind to catch up.

Chapter Fifteen

Sometime later, tightly tied against a tree, DM shivered in the dampness. In every direction more trees seemed to close in on her, but nothing looked familiar. He was right—no one would ever find her here, there'd be no rescue.

"Who are you? Why are you doing this?"

"Do yourself a favor and shut up," her kidnapper said in a raspy voice. He sat on the ground across from her, face sweaty, eyes half-closed. He lit a cigarette and took a long drag. In the dusk, she could barely make out he was bearded with dark shaggy hair.

"Why, if you're planning to kill me anyway?" She bit her lip. "How much money do you want?"

He laughed. "Bet you think you can cure anything with enough cash, don't you? Not this time."

"Look—"

"Save it, bitch. You can think about it all night. I'll be back for you tomorrow." He paused. "Maybe." He stood, stretched and approached her. "Nighty night."

She panicked and shivered more violently as he towered over her. "Please don't leave me here. No, don't—"

Then she felt the prick of a needle in her neck and lost consciousness.

***

"They could be anywhere in these sixty acres," Walsh told Laskey when she arrived at the animal shelter. "Search and Rescue's on the way, but DM's dog, Henry, is our best bet for finding her at this point. I can't believe I lost them."

Laskey handed him an extra flashlight. "He must know this area. Maybe he was the one camping and using the cave. We'll get him."

Walsh sighed. "Yeah, right." He turned to the additional manpower from Cheater's Lake Police. "Follow Henry and his handler in teams of two but spread out. Use the radio to check in."

An hour later with darkness falling and winds increasing, Walsh met again with his team and released them. "We have to suspend the search till morning. It's too dangerous with no light and this coming rainstorm. Everyone meet at the station at six."

Laskey approached him and the two headed for their cars.

"Because Henry's lost the trail—I'm thinking the bastard who took her must have walked here and parked a truck somewhere else. This was obviously planned in advance. And we don't know who he is or what he wants," Walsh said.

Laskey nodded. "But we might have one lead. The crime techs found a cigarette butt on the ground where you stood in line. They get DNA and we can match it —"

"When and if we locate him and hopefully DM's still alive," Walsh interrupted her. "Right now he's calling the shots and we can't do a damn thing about it. Let's call it a day and be ready to hit it hard in the morning." He got into his cruiser, slammed the door and took off down the driveway.

DM was no fool, all she had to do was hang in there. Walsh vowed he'd find her, no matter what it would take.

Chapter Sixteen

DM squinted when mid-morning sunlight hit her eyes. Her thoughts were hazy, confused. They were in an old-fashioned camper and she was at least warm, but her hands and feet were tied.

"I see you're awake, Princess." The man laughed, which turned into a wet cough. "We're gonna have some fun today."

DM could barely move her aching head and now she was gagged. She wanted to scream but wouldn't give him the satisfaction of any reaction, not even a moan. The possibility of choking behind the oily rag he'd shoved in her mouth added to her terror.

"You can think of me as Stan-the-Man. Time to get us some of that great media coverage you crave."

He positioned her against a side bench, arranged himself behind a camera on a tripod. He zoomed in on DM's tear-stained face and the jaunty red bandana rag. "Gorgeous."

Stan recorded his voice with a handheld device.

"Hey, all, this is Daisy Marigold Collins, well-known animal advocate and rich bitch from Seattle. She's in a bad place and needs your donations to save her life. When $10 million appears, she'll come back to you. Till then, she's my toy. Have a good day!"

He finished videotaping with a laugh and cough. Then lit a cigarette, opened a tall can of beer and slurped the liquid. After a few minutes of fiddling with the camera, he bent down on the floor near DM and held up his phone.

"Watch this magic." With a dirt-encrusted fingernail, he played the video, the volume turned high on his distorted voice. He hit Send. The message sped to Seattle TV and newspapers.

***

At the police station a few minutes before six, Detective Mark Walsh and Officer Sharon Laskey met with all available staff. "We have no further news this morning on the DM Collins' case but Search and Rescue wants to hit the area around the shelter again," Walsh said. "All of you are assigned to work in two's the same as yesterday, keep your radios on, and report back here at noon."

After the searchers filed out, Walsh took his hot tea from Laskey and walked down the hall to his office. "You own stock in your coffee shop? I get the idea they never close." He pulled out a chair for her after clearing it of files.

Laskey laughed. "Long story. An old boyfriend of mine runs it and lives in my apartment complex. He does his baking at five, so I hit him up early when necessary."

Walsh rubbed his eyes. "This thing with DM is a mess. The chief's called an old buddy with the FBI, but they need at least a day to clear their own decks and get here. Dammit!"

"She's strong and smart, Boss. Something's bound to break soon."

Walsh's cellphone chirped with a text and attached video. He watched it and yelled, "Son of a bitch!"

***

66

Noontime, against a door in the back, Walsh watched as Chief Riley addressed a group of reporters in the police station conference room.

"As you know, as well as the media, we also received the video from Ms. DM Collins' kidnapper," Riley said into the cameras. "He is demanding $10 million but has not yet supplied any further instructions. If any of your readers or viewers have information about this situation, they should call our tip line immediately."

When the questions began, Walsh slipped out and walked to Laskey's area where she was hard at work on her computer. When she finally paused, he held her coat and motioned to the door. She shut her laptop, took the coat and followed him outside to the parking lot.

***

Walsh drove the cruiser with the window opened partway. "I need some fresh air. How are you holding up?'

"Tired, frustrated. The usual." Laskey glanced around. "Where are we going?"

"To the shooting range. It's time for you to recertify, if you're up for it. Then I'll treat you to a sandwich to celebrate."

She laughed. "Last of the big spenders. I'm okay to shoot. Maybe we can concentrate better out of the station and think of something on DM's case we might have missed."

"Maybe." Walsh slowed for the turn into the range's driveway. "Because her life depends on it."

Chapter Seventeen

Walsh's phone chirped with a text at five the next morning.

"Here's the slightly-worse-for-the-wear, Daisy Marigold Collins. Your pals have had plenty of time to get the $10 million ready. Make sure they're unmarked bills and placed in transparent plastic bags. I'll be in touch later for time and place. And know this, Walsh, I expect you, lover boy, always hanging around her house, to make the drop or the great DM dies a very, very painful death. I'll be sure to forward a keepsake of her last hours."

The video showed a wider shot of DM covered in a camo-colored sleeping bag from the neck down. Her face pale, eyes red and swollen, mouth gagged. Walsh swore and slammed his fist on the bedside table.

In his office an hour later, he replayed the video for Laskey. "I don't get his crack about being her lover. But never mind that. Can you see anything I've missed? I've watched it over and over."

"I don't think—wait. There's a piece of metal at the edge of the sleeping bag. Could it be something from the military?"

Walsh readjusted the focus. He admittedly spent most of his time on DM's face and worrying about her condition. "You might be right. Looks like maybe a Purple Heart." He shook his head. "When the text came in, I called a computer genius in Phoenix to trace the IP address, but he hasn't gotten back to me. Dammit!"

The office clerk, Shawn, entered Walsh's office. He set a tray bearing coffee, tea and pastries on a nearby bookcase. "Got anything I can do to help, Boss?"

"Any idea what happened with the chief's FBI friend?" Walsh took the tea. "Kidnapping is their expertise. We need help now—not when it's convenient for them to get back to us."

Shawn nodded. "I'll follow up on it. The chief's due in at nine," he said on his way out to the hall.

***

At ten o'clock, Laskey opened Walsh's office door at Shawn's knock.

"Chief called in, Boss, he's delayed. He heard his old buddy from the agency died two years ago, so he's left a message with Seattle FBI. Now a couple of people are in the lobby asking to see you about the Collins case."

"I'm on hold for my computer genius. Laskey?"

"I'll check them out." Laskey followed Shawn to the front reception area.

A middle-aged woman in a dark pantsuit stood in the middle of the room, clutching her purse. "Is Detective Walsh in?" she asked.

"He's on the phone." Laskey introduced herself and glanced at a younger man, a Marine, still seated. "How can we help you?"

"I'm Mrs. Clarence Branson," the woman said. "You knew him as Cameron Butts."

"Of course, Mrs. Branson." Laskey thought back to the day she and Walsh examined the caretaker's body after the fire at the animal shelter.

"We're sorry for your loss. Why don't you both come back with me to the break room? We have coffee and it's quieter."

Laskey waited for the Marine to rise. He struggled to pull himself up, cursed, and leaned on a cane. "Just go. I'll catch up," he growled.

After Laskey and the two visitors were settled around a small table, Shawn closed the door and left.

"My son, S-Steven," Mrs. Branson said, her hand holding the Marine's. She squeezed her eyes shut. "This is so difficult."

"Take your time," Steven told his mother.

"You probably know I saw Clarence's photo in the Seattle newspaper a few weeks ago when I attended a notary conference. He'd been gone ten years and we never knew what happened to him. The Chicago FBI came to arrest him and he just ran away. They put my younger daughter, son, and me in Witness Protection. Do you have any idea what that's like, Detective Laskey?"

Laskey didn't bother to correct the woman about her rank. "I can't even imagine."

"We were given a whole new identity and moved to the middle of the country so Clarence's work 'associates' wouldn't be able to kill us. We couldn't even take our dogs, and had to leave all of our friends, relatives and possessions behind. My kids were still in high school! They were supposed to go to college and have a good life. But, thanks to Clarence, things didn't work out that way."

"Mom," the Marine said, "you don't have to tell her all this."

Mrs. Branson got up and dumped her coffee in the sink. "Steven and I think Stan may have kidnapped that Collins woman you're all looking for."

"Stan? I don't understand." Laskey glanced at the Marine. "Your brother?"

"Jesus, Mom, take a breath." He pulled out her chair, patted her arm when she sat. Then he turned to face Laskey. "Yeah, my younger brother. We're worried his finding out about Dad put him over the edge. He's got mental problems."

Walsh stood in the break room doorway. "Stan's a Marine, too?"

Steven didn't reply.

Walsh moved closer to him. "I asked you a question, Marine."

"Yes, sir." Steven met Walsh's eyes, then looked down at his hands. "He always wanted to be like me, his older brother. He enlisted but washed out of basic. Still wears fatigues from the Army & Navy store and spends a lot of his time playing military video games."

"Where is the son-of-a—your brother, now?"

Steven shook his head. "We don't know. We don't even know for sure it's him, but he left a note. Here."

Walsh took the torn piece of lined notebook paper. The message, in small, carefully printed letters, read:

She hid him for 10 years. She's going to pay.

***

Walsh looked up from his paperwork-covered desk at Chief Riley's arrival a few minutes later, accompanied by two men in FBI windbreaker jackets. As usual, Riley didn't bother to knock. "Let's go," he said. Walsh followed the group to the conference room.

Once they unpacked their equipment, the agents immediately set up computers. Walsh traded introductions with the men, repeated the Branson conversation and gave Riley the note from Stan.

Riley scanned the paper. "This case is no longer yours. The agency's in charge of all aspects of the kidnapping and will question the Bransons. Take the rest of the day off."

"But, sir—" Walsh said, jaw clenched.

"Whatever your relationship was with Ms. Collins, it ends now. Out, Detective."

Walsh left.

***

At dinnertime, Walsh carried Greg's duffle bag inside while his friend angled his wheelchair near the couch.

Greg reached over to pet Fred and Ethel, curled together, sound asleep. "So these are the big, bad pussy cats you got stuck with." He laughed. "Pretty fearsome."

"Yeah, yeah. I know, for a better dating image, I should have brought home a huge pit bull, foaming at the mouth. These two can be fearsome when they want. Like in the cave where I found them, and when we were in line to get them fixed..." Walsh paused. "That's funny. It's the only other time they hissed and spit."

"Markie, you might hiss and spit, too, if you were about to be unmanned."

Walsh added more wood to the fireplace. "Once we've eaten, I could use your help with this DM Collins case."

"Sure. Bring on the grub." Greg yawned. "And some coffee. Not that crappy tea you drink. It was a long drive up here with the heavy rain."

Over the next few hours, the men reviewed everything from finding Carson Butts' body to the Bransons' appearance. A few minutes before midnight, they discovered something they'd both missed.

Chapter Eighteen

In his dining room, Detective Walsh cleared remains of bacon and eggs and stacked their plates. "Greg, DM Collins kept meticulous records at the animal shelter." Walsh flipped through several pages and showed his friend two with the same name circled.

"Info on every volunteer, employee, and donor—the usual records for a non-profit. But also visitor logs and everyone who applied to work at the site, whether hired or not."

Greg smiled after he read the printouts. "So, our suspect visited Cheater's Lake Animal Rescue a month before the fire and his father's death. He filled out an application for kennel worker the same day." He poured himself more coffee. "Someone made a note that most of it was illegible except for his name. They couldn't send a thank-you card for applying, just added him to a follow-up list for later. God bless the all-mighty office clerks."

"Yeah," Walsh said, "but we still don't know where the bastard is keeping DM. Thoughts?" He brought over a rolled-up map. "Here's Cheater's Lake."

Greg spread it out on the table. "Best guess is he's camping somewhere on her sixty acres, his idea of another insult. The FBI has resources to search every inch. They've been looking for heat signatures, but the ice storm has helicopters grounded. You gonna call in an update?"

Walsh's phone chimed with a text. "Speak of the devil."

***

Instead, Stan's video featured a side-to-side sweep in a small area of the camper. DM's sleeping bag was empty and there were no other signs of her.

"Okay, Walsh," the distorted voice said, "at 6:00 AM today, take the money to Overlook Bay Park. Leave the plastic bags in the garbage can near the front entrance, the gray one across from the Visitors sign. Then you'll get the feisty Ms. Collins back, maybe in one piece. If anyone else but you shows up, there won't even be any pieces."

Walsh forwarded the video to the chief, FBI agents and Laskey. His phone rang immediately.

"Don't you ever sleep?" Laskey asked.

"You should talk. I'm here at home with Greg. We reviewed every piece of paper in the file, which Shawn copied and slipped into my car. I'm waiting to hear what the Feds want to do now."

Laskey yawned. "What'd you find?"

"You and I followed up on DM's paperwork but we missed a connection. We didn't check again when Carson Butts was identified as Clarence Branson by his widow." Walsh paused. "There's a knock at the door."

"Wait! Tell me what you found and how I can help."

"Laskey," Walsh said, "I'll explain later, but it turns out Stan Branson already knew where his father was before the fire. We have to find him and get DM back." He hung up.

There was a harder knock at the door. "Walsh, it's Steven Branson. Open up!"

Greg drew his weapon and positioned his wheelchair at an angle near the door. "I've got you covered."

Walsh checked the peephole and opened the door. "Come in."

With a grunt, the Marine slowly entered the living room leaning over his cane. "Stan called me a few minutes ago."

"How'd you know where I live?" Walsh said. "And why didn't you just notify the FBI?"

"I followed you home. I don't trust them. I figure you'll do the best you can by my brother."

Greg exchanged looks with Walsh and reversed his chair from the Marine's path. "Tell us what you know."

Branson sighed. "Stan's suicidal. He says he wants to end it, blow up the camper with the two of them in it. I made him tell me where he is—and I can lead you there. We don't have much time. He told me about the money drop."

Chapter Nineteen

"Open up, Stan!" Steven stood at the front door of the camper. "I'm here to help you."

"You better not have anyone with you, man." Stan opened the door far enough to stick out his head. "Don't play me." The tip of his rifle glinted in the early sunlight.

Steven showed his empty hands. Using his cane, he carefully approached his brother. "Is the woman okay?"

Stan pulled him in and locked the door behind him. "Who cares about her? She knew where Dad was for ten years, bro. Ten years!"

"Can I sit?" Steven leaned against the arm of a ratty couch. A woman resembling photos of DM Collins lay across the couch, wrapped in a sleeping bag, still gagged.

"I gotta get the money." Stan pulled on one of Steven's old military jackets. "Borrowed your Purple Heart. Couldn't find mine."

Steven took in Stan's wild eyes, tousled hair and unshaven face. "It's not too late to end this. Come with me and I'll get you help."

Stan shook his head. "All's I need is dough to start a new life. You drive."

"How are you going to hand her over?" Steven asked.

"I'm not. I'll dump her out of the truck. They can find her, or not. Once I get the bags of money, I'll be long gone." Stan opened the door as before, his rifle aimed ahead. "Let's move."

"Wait. How do we get her out? I can't carry her."

Stan sighed. "Take the bag off, untie her legs. She can walk or you can drag her. Stop stalling!"

Steven muttered under his breath to DM. "I'm here to help you." He removed the sleeping bag and untied her legs. "Shake them out and walk beside me."

DM's eyes filled with tears. She gingerly put weight on her feet and swayed.

Stan reached back behind him and grabbed DM. He propped her in front of him. "You can walk, bitch, or die here. Your choice." He glanced at Steven. "Lead the way to my truck."

DM stumbled and nearly fell as Stan prodded her forward. Once at the truck, he nodded to Steven. "Shove her over to the middle of the seat. I know you can drive an automatic with your good leg. I'll hold the rifle on her."

Steven pulled himself into the driver's seat. "Where to?"

Stan gave him directions. "Don't speed, and don't stop if any cop tries to pull us over."

***

Steven drove the sputtering old truck down the icy road at just under the speed limit. He glanced around as they neared Overlook Bay Park, hoping for back up, yet dreading Walsh and the others waiting for them.

"Stop!" Stan screamed. "This is an ambush. I can feel it."

Steven fishtailed the truck to a stop. "There's no one around. What'd you tell them to do?"

"That detective's supposed to leave the money in the trash can."

"Stan, it's not time yet. We can dump the girl and take off, the two of us."

"You'd like that, wouldn't you? Younger brother screws up again." Stan pointed the rifle at him. "Being older than me doesn't mean you're better."

"I know, I—"

Stan fired his rifle, nicking Steven's ear and taking out the driver's window. "Get out before I kill you!"

"Stan, give me the gun!" Steven tried to wrestle it from him.

Stan roared and hit Steven across the head with the rifle butt. He reached over DM and opened the driver's door. "You're a traitor." He shoved Steven out, then pushed DM out of his way and slid behind the wheel. The open door slammed shut as he reversed, then sped away down the blacktop.

***

Walsh and the FBI agents surrounded the unconscious Steven. A paramedic checked him over and he finally came to. "Where'd Stan go?"

"We have people following him at a distance," one of the agents said.

"Great. My brother knows you set up a trap. He'll kill the woman." Steven pushed away the paramedic's hand. "I'm fine, just leave it."

"You have a concussion..."

"Not the first or last time. What's the plan, Walsh?"

Detective Walsh helped Steven sit up. "One of the guys following your brother is a sniper."

"Yeah, Stan knows about snipers. They'll end up killing the woman before they can take him. I'll try talking to him again—I'm the only one he'll listen to. He always listens to me, eventually." Steven pressed his hand against his forehead and the bloodied bandage. "Let's go."

Walsh shook his head. "Bad idea, but I'm not going to stop you. I'll drive." He helped Steven into his cruiser, then yelled to Greg, in his van.

"You got Henry with you?"

He nodded yes.

"Okay, let's move out." Walsh's car skidded on the ice. He got it back on track, Greg following close behind.

"Who's Henry?" Steven asked.

"DM Collins' German Shepherd. He'll find her." Walsh handed a water bottle to the Marine. "You did what you could."

Steven held his head in his hands as the cruiser hit frost heaves and Walsh navigated the treacherous road.

Chapter Twenty

A few miles later, Walsh tapped his brakes and stopped in the middle of the road, inches from Stan's deserted truck, both doors wide open. Dark woods surrounded the area, no houses for miles. An early morning cold mist bathed everything with a thin layer of frost.

Greg pulled his van beside the cruiser and lowered the window. "Now what?' he asked.

"Feels like a set up," Walsh frowned. "We'll give the Feds a couple minutes to get here. Put Henry on his longest lead,"

Steven opened the passenger door. "Stan's most dangerous when he feels cornered. He could shoot us all right now before we decide our next move."

"What's your plan?" Walsh asked.

The Marine stepped out of Walsh's car. "Let me go first." He reached in to grab his cane. "He might listen to me."

Greg motioned to him and handed over Henry's leash. "Take DM's dog. He's the strongest member of our team. I'll stand watch and call for back up."

Within seconds, Henry slipped from Steven's grasp and disappeared into the woods. His bark echoed back as Walsh and Steven attempted to follow the dog through the thick brush.

A scream sounded and swearing. "Get the hell off me!"

The two men moved faster to catch up with Henry, swiping away low hanging branches and slipping on the rough path's icy mud and debris. They finally reached a small clearing.

Stan lay flat on his back under Henry, one arm clamped in strong canine jaws. Whenever he moved, the dog growled, bit deeper.

"Give it up, man!" Steven yelled to his brother.

Stan hollered and struggled to hold on to both DM and his rifle with his good arm. DM, hands tied but legs free, wriggled out of his grip. She kicked Stan's torso to divert his attention from Henry and then lost her balance."

"Kill the dog, bro, or I swear the woman's history." Stan managed to hit at DM's face with the butt of his rifle, momentarily dazing her.

"Stan! A good soldier knows when to stand down." Steven approached him from the side, steering clear of the weapon and the dog.

"I don't take orders from you," Stan gasped. "I said kill the goddamn dog!"

Walsh moved closer and aimed his gun. "When DM's safe, you bastard, we'll call off the dog."

DM stood up and kicked Stan's good arm. He let go of his rifle and punched her leg. She doubled over.

Henry let loose the bloodied arm and latched on to the man's throat. Stan shrieked and tried to shove off his attacker's dead weight.

Steven grabbed at DM's shirt and dragged her away from Stan and the snarling Henry. He removed the gag from DM's mouth, and shouted. "Call your dog off!"

"Henry, drop it!" DM screamed. The dog looked up and ran to his owner.

Able to shift himself, Stan pulled up to a sitting position, grabbed the rifle and pointed it at DM. A hail of gunfire erupted. Blood splattering, he crumpled to the ground.

DM buried her head in Henry's flank and sobbed uncontrollably. Steven took off his jacket and wrapped it around her. "It's all over," he said. "It's all over."

FBI agents swarmed around Stan and roped off the crime scene. Walsh moved a half step toward DM, then turned and headed back to Greg's van, giving him the all-clear on his cell.

Chapter Twenty-One

The next day, Detective Walsh entered the darkened private hospital room as quietly as he could. He carried a cut glass vase with a bouquet of yellow roses which he placed on the tray beside DM's bed.

She stirred and clicked on a lamp as he turned to leave. "Mark, it's so dark. What time is it?"

"Only about six in the evening." He blinked in the bright light.

She smiled. "The flowers are lovely. Yellow roses symbolize forgiveness."

Walsh sat on a small chair next to her bed. "Yeah, I asked the florist. I'm sorry for what happened between us."

DM sat up and ran her fingers through her hair. "Me, too. I know we didn't know each other very well, and you were only doing your job, but it hurt my feelings when you thought I shot Tony Kurtz. You didn't trust me."

Walsh shook his head. "I get it. The timing was wrong for us and I'm sorry I misjudged you. How are you feeling?"

"Tired, can't seem to get warm, and there's at least one nightmare every time I close my eyes to rest. The psychologist Don Santiago hired tells me it's normal after being kidnapped. I still can't believe that guy's dead, but I'm beyond grateful to Henry, you, and Steven." She shuddered.

"DM." Walsh paused when the door opened.

Steven, dressed in civilian clothes, held Henry's leash and limped toward DM. "Oh, sorry. I didn't realize you had company." He nodded to Walsh. "Henry and I took a spin around the grounds after DM fell asleep over dinner. We can go back out again."

"Not necessary." Walsh rose from his chair, then leaned down and kissed DM's cheek. "Take care of yourself." He nodded to Steven and Henry. "The calvary's here. You're obviously in very good hands."

***

An hour later, Walsh and Laskey stood in front of the chief's desk while he paced in the office. "What part of 'you're off the case' did you not understand, Walsh?" Chief Riley said through gritted teeth. "Never mind. I don't want to hear your excuses and lies. You're suspended for two weeks without pay for the officer-involved shooting. Laskey will hand your cases over to me. Both of you get the hell out of my sight."

The two left without a word and walked down the hall. "Greg's leaving in the morning. We want you to join us for dinner tonight," Walsh said.

Laskey smiled. "Sounds good, Boss. I'm dying to hear what went down with Henry and the killer."

"The dog was incredible and so was DM." He opened his office door and grabbed his jacket. "Pizza or Chinese?"

"God, is that all you ever eat? How about a salad?"

Walsh made a face.

"Okay, I'll settle for a sit-down Italian restaurant. You can have pizza. We'll discuss your love life while we dine." They stopped at her cubicle and she gathered her coat and purse.

"If you mean Ms. DM Collins," Walsh sighed, "Steven Branson's her knight in shining armor now. Apparently, Henry's helping him with his PTSD until DM finds another trained dog. Branson deserves it after his war injuries and his brother's death."

"Plenty more fish in the sea, Boss."

"Yup. I won't be fishing in that sea for other women anytime soon. Only kind of fish I'm gunning for now are those in Cheater's Lake. Two weeks of time off is a real gift. Wanna go fishing?" He wriggled his eyebrows.

"Sure." Laskey laughed. "But give me a day or so. I'll bury Riley in paperwork, then join you at the dock. We might find the local fish are really biting."

Walsh opened the exit door. "You know, I got two great cats out of all this and we solved several crimes. Not too shabby."

The door slammed shut behind them as they headed to the parking lot and their vehicles.

THE END

CPSIA information can be obtained
at www.ICGtesting.com
Printed in the USA
FSHW010746200421
80548FS